R.L. STINE

GHOSTS OF
FEAR STREET

FRIGHT KNIGHT

— AND —

THE OOZE

R. L. STINE'S

GHOSTS OF
FEAR STREET ®

FRIGHT KNIGHT

— AND —

THE OOZE

TWICE TERRIFYING TALES

ALADDIN
NEW YORK LONDON TORONTO SYDNEY

This book is a work of fiction. Any references to historical events, real people, or real locales are used fictitiously. Other names, characters, places, and incidents are the product of the author's imagination, and any resemblance to actual events or locales or persons, living or dead, is entirely coincidental.

ALADDIN

An imprint of Simon & Schuster Children's Publishing Division
1230 Avenue of the Americas, New York, NY 10020
This Aladdin paperback edition May 2010
Fright Knight copyright © 1996 by Parachute Press, Inc.
Fright Knight written by Connie Laux
The Ooze copyright © 1996 by Parachute Press, Inc.
The Ooze written by Stephen Roos
All rights reserved, including the right of
reproduction in whole or in part in any form.
ALADDIN is a trademark of Simon & Schuster, Inc., and related
logo is a registered trademark of Simon & Schuster, Inc.
FEAR STREET is a registered trademark of Parachute Press, Inc.
For information about special discounts for bulk purchases, please contact
Simon & Schuster Special Sales at 1-866-506-1949
or business@simonandschuster.com.
The Simon & Schuster Speakers Bureau can bring authors to your live event.
For more information or to book an event contact the Simon & Schuster Speakers
Bureau at 1-866-248-3049 or visit our website at www.simonspeakers.com.
Designed by Karin Paprocki
Manufactured in the United States of America
0410 OFF
2 4 6 8 10 9 7 5 3 1
Library of Congress Control Number 2009931819
ISBN 978-1-4169-9135-9
These titles were previously published individually by Pocket Books.

FRIGHT KNIGHT

"**M**ore blood!" I ordered. I slowly stepped back from the guillotine.

I gazed down at the body kneeling at the bottom of the guillotine. His hands were tied behind his back. I spotted the head on the floor, a few feet away.

The blank eyes stared up at me. The mouth gaped open, frozen in a scream of terror.

I walked over and nudged it with the toe of my sneaker.

"This is nowhere near scary enough," I said.

"Right you are, Mike." Mr. Spellman squirted more fake blood on the wax dummy. A long stream of the sticky red stuff dribbled over the gleaming steel blade of the guillotine.

It looked great—just right for the Museum of History's Mysteries.

"Yu-u-uck!" My sister, Carly, let out one of her earsplitting squeals. She'd been so quiet I had almost forgotten she existed.

No such luck.

She started to jump down from her seat on the old mummy case. Salem, our big black cat, leaped off her lap with an angry meow. Then Carly's feet hit the floor.

"You guys are gross!" She gave us the famous Carly look and rolled her eyes.

Carly has the same blue eyes as me. Her hair is shoulder length and mine is buzzed short for the summer. But it's the same hair. Red. We even have the same freckles all over our noses and cheeks.

My dad has red hair, too. In the pictures I've seen, my mother had brown hair and was kind of small, like me. I don't remember our mom at all. She died when we were really little. For as long as I can remember there's just been Dad, Carly, and me.

I'm twelve and Carly is eleven. We're practically the same height, too. A lot of people think we're twins.

It's enough to make a guy hurl.

My dad says not to worry. Girls grow faster than boys. He promised that someday I'll tower over her.

I dream of that day.

"How can you get so excited over something so

gross?" Carly shivered. "All that phony blood. It's . . . it's—"

"Terrific!" Dad ran into the room. I could tell that he had been dusting the mummies again. Big gunky cobwebs trailed from his clothes. Clouds of dust puffed out of his red hair.

Dad dashed over to the guillotine. He checked it from every angle. His grin grew wider and wider. "Excellent work!"

Mr. Spellman smiled proudly. He took his job as museum caretaker very seriously. Dad gave me and Mr. Spellman the thumbs-up. "But maybe just a little more blood . . ." he added.

Dad took the plastic bottle and squirted a red puddle all around the head. When he was done, he nodded. "Perfect! It's really horrible now."

"Way to go, Dad," I said.

Carly made a soft gagging sound.

He looked right at her. "Don't forget, scary is exactly why people come to Fear Street." Dad's hands were covered with fake blood. He scratched his ear, and a red glob smeared across his face.

Cool! The blood looked even creepier on a live person than it did on a wax dummy. And it will look totally awesome smeared all over me on Halloween.

"That's why the Museum of History's Mysteries is such a stroke of genius." Dad glanced around the old place and smiled.

"I can't fail. Not this time," Dad vowed. "This is the perfect business for Fear Street. It's why we decided to move here to Shadyside in the first place."

I thought back and remembered—remembered the very night Dad got his great brainstorm to move here and open the museum.

So many weird things happen in Shadyside that the town was on the news almost every night. Dad figured people would want to come here and find out for themselves if the stories were true. Which made it the perfect place for a scary museum.

"Where else could you find ghosts playing hide-and-seek in the cemetery?" Dad asked, thinking back to a recent ghost sighting.

"And don't forget that haunted tree house in the woods," Mr. Spellman added.

Dad sighed. "How could I ever forget that?"

I know Mr. Spellman tries to be helpful. But reminding Dad about my friend Dylan and his haunted tree house only made Dad sad. He had missed out on meeting any of the ghosts and was still sort of bummed out about it.

"All we need is something special that people will be . . . well, dying to see." He chuckled at his own joke. "Then people will come. And the Museum of History's Mysteries will be a big success."

"You mean like the alien tracking station you set up

in Grandpa Conway's backyard, Dad?" Carly whined. She didn't give Dad time to answer. She went right on whining.

"Or that freaky petting farm you bought? Let's see—there was the two-headed llama and that stupid unicorn. Couldn't you tell it was a goat with a cardboard horn tied to its head?"

Dad cringed. "I almost forgot about that one," he admitted. "Hey, I thought it was real. Everybody did. It looked real, didn't it, Mike?"

"It looked real to me," I agreed.

Carly made a really mean face at me. I call it her rodent face. It was one of the things she did best.

But I made a better face back at her.

"I think it's going to be great," I said. "All my friends say this place is totally awesome."

"Totally awesome—" Carly imitated me in a squeaky little voice. "Bunch of nerds," she mumbled to herself.

I glared at her. But before I could answer, she turned to my dad again.

"Come on, Dad. What normal kid wants to live in a place that has mummies in the living room and coffins in the dining room and catapults and swords in the kitchen?" she complained.

"How would *you* know what normal kids like, Carly?" I asked.

5

Besides, she wasn't even right. Well, not exactly. All those things were in what used to be the living room and the dining room and the kitchen. That was before Dad turned the downstairs of the big old house into the museum.

We lived upstairs. Our living room, dining room, and kitchen were pretty ordinary compared to down here.

"All right, you two." Dad stepped between us. "No time to fight. Halloween is only two short weeks away. And Shadyside will be crawling with tourists. We've got to be ready for them. We haven't had many customers yet. But Halloween's the perfect time to improve our business." Behind his black-framed glasses Dad's eyes grew serious. I knew what the look meant. He was worried. "They'd better come," he added very quietly. "Or I will have to close."

I knew the thought of closing the museum made Dad sad. It made Mr. Spellman and me sad, too. The Museum of History's Mysteries was a one-and-only kind of place. A place where people could see all sorts of great, spooky stuff. Wax dummies lurked in the basement in the Hall of Wax. Terrifying instruments of torture hung on the back porch. A totally awesome bunch of medieval weapons decorated the front hall. There was no place like it in the whole world.

"Don't worry, Dad," I said. "People will line up and

down the street when that special exhibit gets here from England."

Dad cheered up in a flash. "That's right! Uncle Basil sent it weeks ago. It should be here any day. I can't wait. Imagine how lucky we are! Owning our very own suit of armor!"

I couldn't wait, either. I'm crazy about knights in armor. That was one of the main reasons Mr. Spellman and I were such good friends. He could hardly stop talking about them.

Mr. Spellman worked as the caretaker of the museum since it opened. We have been real close ever since. I couldn't guess his age, but he looked way older than Dad. He was tall and thin. He wore his white hair long, and he had a bushy white mustache. His bright blue eyes lit up whenever he talked about his favorite subjects. Like guillotines or how mummies were made.

He knew everything about really important stuff like that.

Most important, he knew all about knights and swords and castles and dragons.

We talked about knights for hours. He taught me the names of all the weapons—and all about the rules of chivalry. The rules of chivalry told a knight how to behave. How to fight fair. How to be a brave knight.

Mr. Spellman walked over to me and smiled. "And

don't forget," he reminded us, "in his letter, Basil said he was sending along something extra special just for Mike."

Carly didn't need to be reminded. Uncle Basil wasn't sending a present for her.

Her face got all puckery. Like the time we had a contest to see who could eat a whole lemon.

Carly won.

"Aren't you guys forgetting what else Uncle Basil said? That suit of armor is supposed to be haunted!"

"I sure hope so. That's the best thing about it, Carly." Dad wiped the fake blood from his hands with an old rag. "If it is haunted, we're sitting on a gold mine!"

A shiver skipped up my back. The kind of trembly feeling I always felt waiting for something great. My birthday. Or the last day of school.

Or when I felt scared.

But I wasn't scared. I just felt excited. Yeah, that was it. That's why I had a weird, jumpy feeling in my stomach. Sort of like I'd accidentally swallowed a live bug.

"Mr. Conway?" someone called from the front porch. The guy sounded nervous. A lot of delivery and repair people did when they came to the Museum of History's Mysteries. "It's Stanley's Moving and Storage. Got a delivery here for you!"

We all raced out to the front porch. I spotted a giant

moving van parked in front of our house. Two delivery men were pulling a huge crate out of the back. I skidded to a stop in the middle of the porch. Carly slammed into my back. She peered over my shoulder to see what was going on.

The wooden crate had a long, rectangular shape. The rough, dark wood looked very old and knotty. A few of the planks were warped and cracked.

I saw strange-looking stamps all over it. The printing on them looked weird, with strange, twisted letters that I could hardly read. But one big stamp that I could read said FRAGILE in bold red letters.

The delivery men tipped the crate on its side to stand it up. It towered over them.

Dad and Mr. Spellman walked all around it. I scrambled over to them. Carly followed me.

The two delivery guys grunted as they hoisted the crate up on their shoulders. From down where I stood, it looked bigger than ever.

"It's the armor, isn't it?" I asked. I peered through the cracks between the planks of wood, but I couldn't see a thing. I hopped up and down. I couldn't help it. Dad didn't have to answer. I knew his answer from the smile on his face.

"Now be careful. Not too fast. Easy does it, fellas." Dad directed them. "Carry it over to the front porch. We'll drag it inside from there. Carly, out of the way. Mike, you'd better be careful. Not so close. You'll—"

Dad's last words vanished in a kind of choking sound as something sliced through the crate. It gleamed in the sunlight.

It was a giant ax. A knight's battle-ax.

And it came right at me.

The huge blade zipped through the air. As if an invisible hand had taken aim. The blade fell down.

I screamed and jumped out of the way.

But not far enough.

2

"My foot! My foot!"

I took a deep breath. I felt like I was going to hurl.

Then I moved my foot. I wiggled my toes.

My toes?

I forced myself to look down.

The ax blade stuck into the ground. On one side I saw the white rubber toe of my sneaker. On the other side, I saw the rest of my foot.

"Heh, look—" I moved my foot away from the ax. I poked my toes through the hole in my sneaker and wiggled them wildly. They were still attached. All five of them.

My father sighed. A long sigh of relief. I grinned at him.

"It's just the rubber from the shoe, Dad. My toes are fine."

The battle-ax had sliced off the front of my shoe, but I had pulled back my toes just in time. Lucky break for me.

"You've got to be more careful, Mike." Dad slapped my back in that friendly sort of way he always did when he was worried and he didn't want me to know it. "Why don't you go inside and change your shoes."

I didn't want to. I didn't want to miss a second of the excitement. Before I had a chance to start griping, Mr. Spellman put a hand on my shoulder.

"Come on," he said. "Race you to the house."

That was all I needed to hear. I hurried up the steps to the house. I shot under the sign above the door that said MUSEUM OF HISTORY'S MYSTERIES in creepy-looking red letters on a black background. I shoved open the front door and skidded to the right, all set to bolt up the stairs.

I didn't need to. My old sneakers sat on the landing at the bottom of the steps. Right where I was never supposed to leave them.

Mr. Spellman came huffing and puffing into the house. I already had my chopped-up shoes off. I slipped on my old ones.

"Slower than a snail!"

I always said that to Mr. Spellman when I beat him in a race. He usually laughed.

He didn't this time. I don't think he even heard me.

Mr. Spellman looked really excited. His blue eyes lit up. His smile made his bushy white mustache twitch. He plunked down on the step next to me. "Did you see what I saw?" he asked.

He glanced over at the front door. Through the open door we saw Stanley and the other delivery guy coming up the steps with the crate. "Did you read the shipping labels on that crate?"

"Uh, no," I told Mr. Spellman.

"You didn't read them!" he exclaimed in disbelief.

"Give me a break. It's hard to start reading shipping labels when a great big battle-ax is about to split you in two."

"Okay, okay. Those labels say that the armor was shipped from Dreadbury Castle." Mr. Spellman rubbed his hands together. "This is even better than I thought, Mike. Much better."

"It is?"

"If I remember my history right . . ." Thinking really hard, Mr. Spellman squeezed his eyes shut. "Yes. That's right. That's it!" He hopped to his feet. "Dreadbury Castle was the home of Sir Thomas Barlayne!"

He announced the name as if it was supposed to mean something to me.

It didn't.

Mr. Spellman shook his head. "Don't you remember the story of Sir Thomas Barlayne? Sir Thomas was an evil knight. A wicked knight. Some say he was the most wicked knight who ever lived. Finally a noble wizard cast a spell on Sir Thomas. He trapped the wicked knight inside his suit of armor forever."

I stood up. "But that's good, isn't it? That's just what Dad wants. A haunted suit of armor for the museum."

"Yes, that's what your dad wants." Some of the excitement faded from Mr. Spellman's eyes. His voice dropped low. "I wonder if he knows the rest of the story."

He might have been talking to himself, but he sure got my attention.

I grabbed Mr. Spellman's sleeve and tugged. "Rest of what story?"

Mr. Spellman laughed. "Oh, nothing much," he said. He waved away my question with one hand. "It's just some silly old story. According to the legend, whoever owns Sir Thomas's armor is cursed. He's doomed to bad luck—or worse!"

"Worse?" The word squeaked out of me. Bad luck, I could imagine. I could picture getting F's on math tests even though I studied. I could imagine my friend Pete telling the whole world I had a crush on Sara Medlow. And I sure could picture being Carly's brother.

All that was bad luck.

But worse?

"But if the legend is true, won't that be great for the museum?"

Mr. Spellman looked down at me. His eyes twinkled. His mustache twitched. "Maybe not so great for us, huh?"

He bent down so that he could look right into my eyes. "I'll tell you what, Mike. Let's keep this our secret, okay? There's no use worrying your dad. And we don't want to scare Carly. If the armor is haunted . . ."

He straightened up and looked out the window. "What do you say we play detective?"

"You mean we'll check it out together?"

Mr. Spellman nodded.

"Excellent!" He slapped me a high five. "And don't worry, Mr. Spellman," I told him. "I'll watch out for you."

"And I"—Mr. Spellman ruffled my hair—"will watch out for you. Deal?"

"Deal!"

We walked outside onto the porch together. We both smiled about our secret pact. I saw the delivery guys climbing back into their truck. Then I saw the crate stretched out beside me.

Dad didn't waste any time. Holding a crowbar, he crouched down next to the crate. He slipped the edge of the bar under the crate's lid and pushed. I heard a squeaking sound as the nails that held the lid in place came loose.

As Dad pushed up with the crowbar, Mr. Spellman grabbed the edge of the lid and pulled. Carly stood to one side. She was pretending she didn't care much. But I noticed that she was chewing on her lower lip. Her nervous habit.

I sort of hopped around the crate in the circle. I felt so excited I couldn't keep still.

Finally Dad and Mr. Spellman lifted the lid off the crate. I scooted forward. I held my breath. Carly stood right next to me.

We all leaned over and peered inside.

All I saw were piles and piles of fluffy stuff. Shredded newspaper.

"It's paper." Carly sounded as disappointed as I felt.

Dad grinned. "Not just paper, Carly," he said. "Go ahead. Reach in there and see what you can find."

"Me?" Carly squeaked.

"Are you afraid?" Dad asked.

"No way," she said. I could tell she was scared silly. But acting like everything was cool.

The long crate suddenly reminded me of a coffin. I wondered if Carly had the same idea, too.

Her mouth twitched. She pushed up the sleeve of her blue sweater. She reached into the crate. Her arm disappeared into the mountains of paper shreds.

The paper rustled as she felt around for something solid. I saw her lean over and reach in even deeper.

"I think I feel something," she told us.

Then she screamed.

"It's got me! It's grabbed me! Help!"

I watched Carly try and try again to yank her arm out.

But something—or someone—had grabbed her.

And it wouldn't let go.

3

Carly tugged and squirmed. Her face turned red. Dad and Mr. Spellman started digging. Shredded newspaper flew in all directions.

"Hold on now, honey," Dad said.

"Hurry! It's got me," she wailed.

She was out of control. Even I felt sorry for her. Well, almost.

Dad pulled up her arm. The fingers of a metal hand were wrapped around Carly's wrist.

"Well, would you look at this," Dad said. He laughed. The metal hand was attached to a long metal arm.

"Your bracelet got caught," Dad said. "Hold still. I'll have you unhooked in a second." He pried the metal fingers open one by one. Carly snatched back her hand.

The metal hand and arm dropped back into the crate with a clunk.

"Stupid armor," Carly grumbled. She looked down at her wrist, rubbing it.

I looked over my shoulder at Mr. Spellman. I rolled my eyes. He rolled his, too.

Dad reached in and pulled out another piece. "Now look at this," he said.

Smiling, Dad held up a helmet. The last rays of the setting sun glinted against the metal, turning it glowing red. Hot. Fiery.

My mouth fell open. I didn't even realize I was holding my breath until I let it go. "Cool! It's so cool."

Then Dad handed the helmet to me. Just looking at the helmet was nothing compared to touching it.

I ran my hands over it. It felt heavier than I thought it would. And not cold. Not like metal should be. It felt warm. The way it would be if somebody had just taken it off.

A shiver crawled up my back. I cradled the helmet in my arms. Dad pulled a metal shin guard out of the crate and set it on the floor. A metal foot guard came next.

Dad's eyes gleamed. He reached into the pile of shredded paper for another piece of the armor. "This is it! Our chance at fame and fortune. This is going to be the best and the spookiest exhibit anyone has ever seen. On Fear Street or any place else. People will come from all over the world to see it and—"

His words stopped suddenly. His sandy-colored eyebrows drew together as he frowned. He kept moving his hand around under the shredded paper. He felt around for something way down at the bottom of the crate.

"What's this?" Dad pulled his arm out. He held up something bright and shiny. The strange round object dangled at the end of a long golden chain.

It looked like a giant marble, but weirder looking than any marble I had ever seen.

Inside the marble strange blue smoke spiraled and swirled. Dark blue. Light blue. Sparkling silvery flecks whirled slowly around in the smoke, like tiny shooting stars.

I grabbed for it.

So did Carly.

So did Mr. Spellman.

I got there first.

"Slower than snails!" I grinned at them, the pendant in my hands. "This must be my special surprise from Uncle Basil!" I slipped the chain over my neck before anybody else had a chance to touch it. I stared down at the pendant dangling against my white T-shirt. "Gee—it looks cool, doesn't it?"

Dad agreed. So did Carly. She sounded jealous. That made me like the pendant even more.

Mr. Spellman stepped forward. "If you ask me," he said, looking at the pendant, "it looks positively magical."

"Yeah, it does sort of, doesn't it?" I nodded.

A magic pendant.

It was the best surprise I'd had since Dad took us to New York City last year to buy a new mummy.

We all watched as Dad finished unpacking the crate. We gathered up the armor and took it into the front hall.

Mr. Spellman and I handed Dad the pieces. Piece by piece, he slowly put Sir Thomas together.

Carly stood by, holding Salem in her arms. I could tell she didn't want to touch the armor.

When Dad finished, we all stood back and took a good look.

Sir Thomas's armor could have easily fit my favorite pro wrestler, Hulk Hooligan. The shoulders were about a yard wide. The legs were round and solid. They reminded me of small tree trunks. About three of me could have hidden behind the breastplate, no problem.

I thought about all the stories in all my books about castles and knights.

"Awesome!" I let out the word at the end of a sigh.

"He does look awesome, doesn't he?" Mr. Spellman clapped me on the back.

Dad smiled. "Now all we have to do is keep our fingers crossed. If we're lucky, this old pile of metal really is haunted. And that will bring the customers running!"

The phone rang and Dad went to answer it. Mr. Spellman hurried out, too. He said he had some work to do down in the wax museum. When they were gone, Carly edged up real close to me.

"What do you think, Mikey?" She always calls me Mikey when she tries to make me mad. "Are you scared the armor might really be haunted?"

"The only thing I'm scared of is your ugly face!" I gave her a playful punch on the arm. Then I dashed out of the hall and up the stairs.

It was my turn to start dinner. I knew exactly what I was going to make—macaroni and cheese, the food Carly hated more than anything in the whole wide world.

It was Carly's turn to do the dishes. I made sure I cooked the macaroni and cheese just a little too long. So after dinner she had to scrape all the hard pieces off the bottom of the pan. While she was doing that and grumbling to herself, I hurried to my room.

I still had a school project to do about polar bears. I had to read the report to my class tomorrow. Also my favorite TV show, *Scream Theater,* was on at nine.

I did my homework, but I never got a chance to watch *Scream Theater*. It had been a big day. I was beat.

I brushed my teeth, pulled on my pajamas, and fell into bed.

But I kept my pendant on. Stretched out in bed, I held it up in front of my face. I watched the curling blue smoke glimmer in the moonlight that slipped through my window blinds.

I got this weird feeling that the smoke was hiding something. Something really great. I tried to get a closer look. But the more I looked, the more the color swirled.

I fell asleep before I knew it.

Thump. Thump.

I was dreaming about something. I couldn't remember what. I thought it had something to do with polar bears. And blue marbles. And knights in shining armor.

Thump. Thump.

There it was again.

I opened my eyes and listened.

Thump. Thump.

Definitely not part of my dream.

I sat up and held my breath.

Thump. Thump.

It came from downstairs.

Thump. Thump.

I swung my legs over the side of the bed. I sat with my head tilted, listening closer.

Thump. Thump.

I couldn't think of anything down in the museum that made that kind of noise.

At least, not before tonight.

Thump. Thump.

I stood up. My legs felt a little rubbery.

Only one thing could be making the noise.

The armor.

Thump. Thump.

I gulped and hurried downstairs. The museum kitchen was right under my room. The closer I got to it, the louder it sounded.

Thump. Thump.

I gazed down at my pendant. The swirling blue smoke pulsed to the rhythm of the sounds.

Thump. Thump.

I moved through the museum, following the sound. At the door to the kitchen, I stopped. I gulped for air, the way I do in gym class when Mr. Sirk, our PE teacher, makes us run extra laps.

This was it! My chance to catch a ghost in action. My chance to prove that the armor really was haunted!

Thump. Thump.

I took a deep breath. I pushed open the kitchen door.

Thump. Thump.

I took a couple of shaky steps inside.

Thump. Thump.

I squinted into the dark. And I saw it.

It was hideous.

I couldn't help it. I screamed.

4

"Carly! You creep!"

My jerky sister stood in the middle of the kitchen with a broom in her hands. She pounded on the ceiling with the handle.

I glared at her. "What do you think you're doing?" I tried to keep my voice down. I didn't want to wake Dad.

Carly was doubled over laughing. She pointed at my face. "Look, it's the nerd patrol. Out ghost hunting."

Carly laughed some more. She can really crack herself up with her dumb jokes.

"Yeah, well, only a true jerk starts banging a broom handle on the ceiling in the middle of the night," I said.

I fingered my blue pendant. Now that the thumping had stopped, the pulsing had stopped, too. I closed my fingers around it.

"You're lucky Dad didn't wake up," I told her. "He would have thought the ghost had come for sure. He would have been so excited. Can you imagine how he would have felt when he found out it was only you?"

For once, Carly actually looked sorry. She put down the broom. "I guess I never thought of that," she said. "I just wanted to scare you."

"Well, you didn't." I crossed my arms over my chest. I tried to give her the same kind of look Dad gave us when we made him angry or disappointed. "You just caused trouble, that's all."

I suppose I should have considered myself lucky. I had actually seen Carly look sorry for once. I should have known it would never happen again.

"What's the matter, Mikey? Were you afraid of the big, bad knight down here?"

"Look who's talking. You're the one who thought it grabbed you," I reminded her. "O-o-oh! Help me! Help me!" I imitated her in a high-pitched, girl voice.

"Well, I'm not scared now," she said. She tossed her hair over one shoulder. "You're the one who believes in haunted armor."

"Well, what if the legend is true?" I asked her. "Do you want to meet the ghost of the most wicked knight who ever lived?"

"Oh, come on," Carly said. "You don't believe all that stuff? I mean, you don't think the armor could . . . could walk around or anything, do you?"

"There's only one way to find out."

Carly pretended that she didn't care about the haunted armor and the curse. But I could tell that deep down inside, she was scared.

But I wasn't scared.

"Come on." I grabbed her arm and pulled her out of the kitchen. "Let's go check it out."

As we left the kitchen and turned down the dark hallway, I started to get that creepy feeling again.

Not that I'm a chicken or anything. But the Museum of History's Mysteries can be sort of spooky. Especially at night.

In the moonlight that poured through the windows, our shadows looked all twisted and deformed. And things around the place you normally didn't notice, like a lamp or a big potted plant, looked a lot different in the dark—like they might reach out and grab you.

I heard a *squeak, squeak, squeak.* It sounded like fingernails on a blackboard. It made my skin crawl.

I stopped.

The noise stopped.

It was only the floor. I sighed.

I should have known. Everything around the museum always squeaks. It's part of what makes the big old house so much fun.

Except at night. When you're creeping through the place all alone with no one but your goofy sister. And you're looking for a haunted suit of armor.

We reached the dining room, where Dad's entire coffin collection is on display. He likes to call the room Coffin Central. He thinks that's pretty funny.

In the daytime it's a great place to play hide-and-seek.

But at night . . .

I heard a small hiccup. Then I realized I had made it. I glanced over at Carly, waiting for her to tease me.

But for once, Carly didn't say a word. I guess the room had creeped her out, too. She grabbed my hand. Her steps dragged.

I pulled her into the room. All the coffins were closed. Mr. Spellman always closed them before he went home at night.

What did it matter? Both of us knew what each and every one of them held.

The one next to us held a wax dummy of Dracula. Wooden stake through the heart and all.

The one over on our right had a wax dummy inside, too.

But the dummy had a mirror in place of a face. When you bent over the coffin and looked inside . . .

A shiver snaked its way up my back and over my shoulders. I walked a little faster.

"You're not scared, are you, Mikey?" This time

Carly wasn't teasing me. I could tell she was hoping I'd say no.

"No way." Was that me talking so tough? I tried to keep my voice steady. "There's nothing to be afraid of—

"Yow!" I let out a yelp of pain. Carly grabbed my arm.

"Mike? What? What?"

"I banged my knee on a coffin." Ouch. I rubbed my leg. "That hurts."

"Try not to be such a klutz," she whispered. "You'll wake up Dad."

"Try not to be such a chicken."

"Me? I'm not afraid of anything," she said.

"Except the haunted armor," I reminded her.

I kept walking, but Carly stopped in her tracks. I glanced back at her. She stood frozen to the spot. She peered into the shadows, twisting a strand of hair with her fingers.

"Maybe this isn't such a great idea after all. I mean . . ." Carly said in a shaky voice, "what if there really is a ghost? Maybe we should give him a few nights to sort of rest and get used to the place."

I didn't bother answering. Mostly because I hoped there *was* a ghost. And a curse. I wanted people to come to see Sir Thomas from miles around so we would make a zillion dollars and could live in the museum forever.

We finally made it through the coffin room and went into the living room. Even though Dad had spent the entire afternoon dusting the mummies, dust covered every inch of everything else. Clouds of dust drifted over the floor and blew around our feet as we walked.

That's exactly the way Dad likes it.

Dusty and musty. With cobwebs hanging off the walls like ghoulish party streamers.

As we crept across the floor, our slippers made a dull scraping sound. The sound a mummy might make dragging itself across the room.

Mr. Spellman always closed the coffins at night. But the mummies were always open for business.

Out of the corner of my eye I could see Dad's favorite mummy. The one he called Charlie. Charlie stood propped up in his case. His stiff arms jutted out in front of him. His sunken eyes stared across the darkness. Right at us.

I made a gulping sound and tried to cover it up with a cough.

"Race you the rest of the way!" I dropped Carly's hand. I sprinted into the parlor. Dad had set up the armor on a wooden stand just inside the doorway.

I beat Carly by a mile and stopped near the open door, waiting for her.

Finally she caught up. I grinned. "Slow as a snail!"

Carly didn't answer.

She stared over my shoulder. Her mouth dropped open.

She pointed.

I looked through the doorway and saw—nothing.

Empty space.

The armor was gone!

5

"**M**ike!" Carly's voice trembled. "Mike, where is he? Where is the knight?"

He had vanished all right. All that remained of him was his wooden stand.

"Do you know what this means?" I asked her.

"Yeah." Carly gulped. "The armor moved. It really is haunted."

"Right! The story is true!" I whispered. "Sir Thomas's ghost is in that armor. And he can move! He can walk!"

"He could be anywhere!" Carly croaked. "He could be hiding in the basement. He could be on his way upstairs." She took a step back into the mummy room. "He could be right in this room. Hiding in the dark."

I scanned the shadows. "I don't think so," I told her. "He's pretty big. I think we'd notice him. Let's look for him."

"Maybe he'll come back on his own," she replied in a shaky voice. "Like Salem does when he sneaks out of the house at night."

"Carly, get real. We're talking about a ghost, okay?"

I grabbed a handful of her robe and dragged her back the way we came. We already knew Sir Thomas wasn't in the mummy room. He wasn't in the coffin room. I didn't look too closely at the dark shadows in the kitchen, but I felt pretty sure he wasn't in there, either.

"Let's check out the wax museum."

"No way!" Carly hates the wax museum. She squinched up her eyes. "Anywhere but the wax museum!"

"All right." I paused and thought about where a ghost might be lurking. "How about the conservatory?"

Before Carly could think of some dumb excuse, I led her toward the back of the house.

When we first moved into the house on Fear Street, it took me a long time to figure out what a conservatory was. Dad finally explained that it was a sort of greenhouse. The huge, empty, roller rink–size room had a glass ceiling and glass walls on one end. The original owners of the house used to grow all kinds of plants in there, even in the winter.

Dad hardly ever used the conservatory for museum exhibits. It was way too big. And really needed some repairs.

We pushed open the door and went inside. Eerie blue moonlight shone down through the glass walls and domed roof.

We crept along, close to the wall, and then ducked under the tropical plants Dad planned to use in the mummy exhibit. I peered through the big, floppy leaves. Something up ahead flashed and sparkled.

Like moonlight glinting off armor.

With one finger on my lips, I signaled Carly to keep quiet. We tiptoed through the shadows side by side. A cobweb trailed across my face. I brushed the sticky web aside. And caught my breath.

Sir Thomas! There he was.

He sat on a full-size model horse, right in the middle of the conservatory. The high glass dome arched above him.

I blinked.

For a second I thought I saw him move.

I blinked again.

I took a step closer.

"Awesome!" My voice echoed in the big empty room.

A high ladder stood next to the model horse. The ladder Dad always used to set up his exhibits.

"See? You were scared for nothing." I knew I didn't have to whisper anymore. "Dad and Mr. Spellman must have done it. They must have moved the knight in here when we were doing our homework."

I noticed then that they had also moved most of Dad's medieval weapons in here, too. Almost his entire collection. About a dozen lances hung on the wall to the left of the knight. And on the wall to the right of the knight I saw a display of big metal swords and shields.

Propped up in the corner, I spotted Dad's fake suit of armor, too. He'd bought it for a display in the museum and it had all the details of real armor. It even looked real from a distance. But close up you could tell it was made of cheap, thin tin.

I'd always loved that fake armor. But now that we had the real thing, it didn't look like much.

"Looks like they brought a lot of stuff in here," I said.

Carly wrinkled her nose. "Why?"

"Why?" A Carly question if I ever heard one. "Probably because there's more room in here. More people will have a chance to see the armor and all the cool weapons a knight like Sir Thomas needed to fight his enemies."

I stared up at Sir Thomas again. "He's awesome, isn't he?"

"Yeah, awesome," she echoed halfheartedly.

Seated on the horse, Sir Thomas appeared ready to fight. He carried a long, pointy lance in one hand. His other hand wrapped around the horse's reins. In that same hand he also grasped a shield.

The ghostly white moonlight flickered off Sir Thomas's helmet. It sparkled against his lance. It made the armor glow with a powerful green light. Glow from the inside.

It was the coolest thing I ever saw in my whole, entire life. I wanted to get as close as I could. Really, really close.

I walked toward him.

"Mike, what are you doing?"

Over my shoulder I saw Carly take a step back. "Dad might not like it if you—"

"Dad won't mind."

Oh, yes, he would, a little voice inside said. *He'd mind big-time. You'll be grounded for the rest of your life if he catches you messing around with that armor.*

But I'm not going to mess with it, I answered the voice. *I only want a closer look. Just one tiny peek. I've got to see where that green glow is coming from. Dad will understand.*

"It's truly excellent, isn't it?"

I don't know if Carly answered me or not. I wasn't listening.

All of a sudden I had to touch the armor.

I stood really close now. I stretched up as far as I could. That didn't help much. Sir Thomas sat on his horse. And the horse stood on a platform. Like I said, I'm sort of short.

Hey, but that's what ladders are made for, right? I grabbed the ladder and started climbing up.

"Mike, you're not going to—"

I ignored Carly. I ignored everything. Everything but the weird feeling that traveled down my arms. Tingling in my fingers.

I climbed to the very top of the ladder.

From up there the armor looked better than ever. I caught my breath. I studied the fancy designs on the breastplate and helmet. There were even a couple dents. I figured Sir Thomas got those in battle.

I gazed at the visor. The part the knight raised so he could eat and talk.

I gazed into the slit above the visor. The space where the knight looked out. It looked dark and empty.

I hooked my left arm around one side of the ladder. Then I leaned out as far as I could. My fingers brushed Sir Thomas's helmet.

The tingling got stronger.

"See. Nothing to worry about." I glanced down. Carly stared up at me. Her eyes were round. Her mouth hung open. "I bet I can even get a look inside."

Stretching out really far, I hooked my finger around the bottom of Sir Thomas's visor. I nudged it open.

The visor squeaked.

It didn't squeak like the museum floor squeaked. That was a friendly kind of squeak.

This squeak made my bones vibrate. It made my teeth ache.

The ladder wobbled. I steadied myself.

Before I even realized it, I stood face-to-face with the helmet.

Nothing to see. Nothing but a blackness. Blacker than the night.

I leaned over farther and peered inside. Blackness. Thick, dense.

I caught a whiff of something putrid—a pile of old garbage that had been around awhile. Say, a few centuries.

I felt sick to my stomach.

Then I heard a long groan. Like someone moaning from the other end of a long tunnel.

The sound grew louder. It filled my head. It drowned out the noisy *whoosh* of the blood rushing in my ears.

I leaned back and felt the ladder wobble under me. My entire body broke out in gooseflesh.

Something was moving. Inside the helmet. Something was coming. A black shadow!

The shrieking and moaning grew louder. And louder.

The armor trembled. Then shook violently.

With a ghastly cry that chilled my bones, the shadow rose up out of the armor.

I was done for.

6

The shadow rose out of the armor and came straight at me.

With my eyes squeezed shut, I heard a creepy sound of fleshy wings flapping around my head and neck.

I swatted wildly at the air. Then it flew around my head and dived at me from the other side.

I tried to duck. Too late.

The biggest, blackest, ugliest bat that ever lived flew right into my face.

I stared into two terrifying glowing red eyes. The bat's horrid mouth opened, baring sharp fangs. I saw its wicked claws flex. Ready—ready to dig into me.

I swung my arms over my head as the bat swooped at me again. Big, creepy wings flapped against my ear.

"Whoa!" I yelped. I lost my balance and fell backward off the ladder.

I landed on the floor with a thud. I felt like a bug hitting a car windshield.

"Are you all right?" I looked up and saw Carly standing over me. She offered me a hand up.

With a loud grunt I pulled myself to my feet. All my bones seemed to be in one piece. But just barely. I'd lost one of my slippers, and my pajamas had twisted all around my legs.

"Have a nice flight?" Carly asked sweetly.

"Very funny." I dusted off the seat of my pajamas. I spotted my missing slipper over by Sir Thomas's horse. I grabbed it and slipped it on. "That bat had to weigh at least fifty pounds. Its wings stretched out about a yard."

Carly made a face. "Bats! Yuck! Where did it go? Is it still here?" She covered her head and stared at the ceiling.

"I don't know," I said. "It just flew away."

Carly glanced at the ceiling again. "I don't know about you, but I'm going back to bed."

"Go ahead." I stepped back to let her by.

I watched Carly quickly walk out of the conservatory. She disappeared into the shadows on the far side of the room. A minute later I heard the sounds of her footsteps as she climbed the stairs.

I sighed. It was late. I had school tomorrow. First thing in the morning I had to give my report. I hoped I didn't nod out right in the middle of it.

Staying up suddenly seemed like a huge waste of time.

Had I found a ghost?

No.

All I found was my stupid sister.

And a bat.

I sighed. Pretty disappointing. I headed for the door. My slippers scuffed across the floor.

But about halfway across the room I thought I saw something. Out of the corner of my eye.

Something moving.

Metal flashing in the moonlight.

I stopped and squinted through the shadows at the armor.

Wasn't Sir Thomas staring in the *other* direction the last time I looked at him?

I shook my head. I rubbed my eyes.

No. Couldn't be.

Right?

The question tapped at my brain. My insides suddenly quivered. I decided to get out of the conservatory. Fast.

My racing footsteps slapped against the tile floor.

My heart pounded against my ribs.

At the door I quickly glanced back at Sir Thomas. He was right where he belonged.

I let out a deep breath and started the long trek to the stairs.

I crept through the kitchen, finding my way by the light of the moon. A cold, spooky glow flowed through the windows.

The moonlight shimmered against a huge, old broadsword hanging on the wall. Next to the sword hung a set of heavy chains. The links looked like teeth.

Hungry teeth. Grinning at me.

I couldn't help it. I shivered.

Get a grip, I told myself. You're acting like a dweeb. A total nerd. This is the Museum of History's Mysteries, right? It's home, right? What are you scared of?

I didn't stop to answer myself. I just walked a little faster.

The coffin room looked exactly the way we had left it.

Or did it?

The lid on Dracula's coffin . . . I didn't remember it being open like that. Just a tiny crack.

I didn't stop to check it out. I dashed into the mummy room.

I saw good old Charlie. Right where he always stood. His eyes still stared their mummy stare. His arms still jutted out straight. Mummy fingers dangling.

Reaching for me as I rushed past.

A flutter in the pit of my stomach told me not to think about that.

But by then it was too late.

My head whirled. I took a deep breath.

And choked on a mouthful of mummy dust.

I needed fresh air. Fast.

I bolted out of the mummy room. Up ahead I saw the doors that led out of the museum. The doors in the parlor. I sprinted toward them, coughing and gasping.

Air. I needed air.

The doors are the big, double kind. The kind they have at school. They have those metal handles that you press down to open. I grabbed the door handle and pressed.

The door didn't move.

I tried again. I pushed against it with my whole body.

Nothing. The door didn't budge an inch.

I dragged my hand over the wall. I felt the light switch and flicked on the overhead lights. Something told me I wasn't going to like what I saw.

My breath caught in my throat. It was a knight's sword.

Someone had jammed it right through both sets of door handles.

I threw myself against the doors and pulled and pulled at the sword. It was heavy. It didn't budge.

I was trapped!

7

"**T**rapped."

I heard my voice echo in the emptiness all around me.

I stood up again and wrapped both my hands around the cold, hard handle of the sword. I took a deep breath and pulled again.

Harder and harder.

My arms ached and blood pounded in my head.

No use.

Panting, I beat the sword with my fists.

Nothing.

I backed up and gave the door and the sword a ninja kick.

My foot throbbed with pain. But the sword didn't even jiggle.

Trapped.

This time the word echoed inside my head.

I had to backtrack. Through the entire museum. Through the mummy room. The coffin room. And the creepy kitchen.

I had to go through the conservatory. I had to reach the back door at the far side of that room. Or else . . . I stopped myself from thinking that far. I didn't want to think about the evil knight. Not now.

"I can't be trapped. I can't be trapped. I can't be trapped."

I chanted the words out loud as I ran through the dark shadowy rooms.

"How could I be trapped? Carly went out that way. Just a couple minutes ago. There's no way anyone could have stuck that sword in the door since then. I would have seen them. Sure. Yeah. That's right. No way. I would have seen them for sure."

I kept walking and talking out loud to myself. And I hung on to my blue marble pendant. I'm not sure why. But I felt better when I was holding it. Braver.

I stopped at the conservatory door. I opened it a crack and peeked inside.

Sir Thomas was still there—sitting on his horse. Just like when I left him.

I didn't breathe a sigh of relief. I don't think I

breathed at all. The whole time. I held my breath as I brushed under Dad's weird plants. I held my breath as I hurried past the ladder.

When I got all the way past Sir Thomas and nothing happened, I finally let the breath go. I didn't slow down, but the knots in my stomach loosened up a little.

The back door loomed closer. And closer. I walked faster. And faster. It came closer still.

Almost in reach now.

Then I heard a strange sound.

A creaking sound.

Shivers raced up my arms and legs. My knees wobbled.

I told myself, "Keep walking. Do *not* turn around and look."

The creaking grew louder.

But I had to look. I couldn't stop myself.

I turned very slowly.

What I saw made me freeze in place. My heart stopped.

The suit of armor.

Standing right behind me. Towering over me.

How did it get off the horse?

I took a gulp of air and forced myself to look up.

Through the slit above the visor I saw a fiery red glow. When my gaze met that glow, it grew brighter. Hotter. Redder.

Then I knew.

Sir Thomas. He was in there.

The armor creaked as he took a step closer.

I felt myself stumbling backward. The room spun.

"I . . . I . . . I . . ." I sputtered, trying to stay on my feet. Never taking my gaze off him for a second.

Then with the scraping sound of metal against metal, Sir Thomas raised one hand. He pointed right at me.

I stopped sputtering. My mouth hung open.

"You!" His deep voice boomed from inside the suit of armor. "You will not escape me this time, evil wizard!"

8

"**M**e? A wizard?" I choked out the words.

"Wait a second," I sputtered. "I'm just a sixth grader at Shadyside Middle School. Ask anybody. I'm no wizard."

"Save your wizard's lies for fools!" Sir Thomas's words boomed all around me.

The glass dome above us rattled and groaned, as if blasted by a huge gust of wind.

"It is your doing, wicked one. You and your magic trapped me in this metal tomb with your evil magic."

"Me?" I shook from head to toe. My pendant swung back and forth across my chest. The blue smoke inside it swirled.

"You've got me mixed up with somebody else. Honest. I've never even seen you before today, Sir Thomas. Sir Thomas, sir, I mean—" I added. Grown-ups usually like it when you act all polite. I figured it was worth a try.

No such luck.

"Vile one!" he roared. The fire behind Sir Thomas's visor grew bloodred and flickered. He tilted his head to take a closer look at me.

The next second I heard a furious snarl. Moving way faster than a guy should have been able to move wearing a couple hundred pounds of armor, Sir Thomas raised his lance. He lunged at me. He held the point of it right at my throat. "Prepare to die, hateful wizard!"

The needle-sharp lance pricked my skin. The metal felt fiery hot.

He wanted to kill me.

Slice me in half.

Chop me up in little pieces. And then even smaller pieces after that.

I didn't stand a chance against him.

I swallowed hard and took a giant step back.

Sir Thomas rattled forward. He snarled again. The flames behind his visor flickered and hissed.

"Did you think you could fool me by taking the shape of a young boy?" Sir Thomas roared at me. "I fought you when you turned yourself into a dragon. I fought you when you changed yourself into a wall of fire. And now . . ."

The knight dug the lance tip into my skin. "Now, wizard, I will have my revenge!"

I tried to scream for help. I tried to scream for Dad. Or even Carly.

I croaked pathetically.

Sir Thomas dipped his head and made a deep metallic grinding sound.

I took a couple of steps back.

The knight took a couple steps forward. He tossed his lance away. It clattered to the floor.

Great! He finally believes me, I thought.

Then he stepped even closer.

"I have waited centuries for this moment, wizard. I want to see your evil eyes as you gasp for your dying breath," his deep voice bellowed.

I stared up at him, frozen with fear. I couldn't move. I backed toward a corner. No place to hide. And I knew I'd never get past him alive.

Dad had set up a whole bunch of medieval weapons around the horse. Too bad for me. Sir Thomas had his pick.

"Should I use the broadsword?" Sir Thomas grabbed for it. "Or the mace?" He picked up the mace in his other hand.

He swiped the big, heavy sword through the air. In the moonlight the sharp blade gave off an icy glint.

Then he held out the mace at arm's length.

Sir Thomas's mace looked like a big club. Studded with spikes all around the top. Metal spikes filed to needle-sharp points.

They sparked at me. They flashed.

I cringed. I imagined what they would feel like biting into my skin.

"Chivalry!" I screamed the word. I forced myself to sound brave.

"You call yourself a knight? A real knight wouldn't attack an unarmed person. A real knight wouldn't go against the code of chivalry. Mr. Spellman said so."

The red glow behind the visor flickered.

"You are correct, foul wizard," Sir Thomas admitted. "I cannot attack an unarmed man." He stepped back and swept his arm out over Dad's display of weapons. "Choose."

My hands shaking, my heart pumping, I looked over the weapons. Could I save myself with any of them? Not likely. I picked up a heavy shield. One big enough to hide behind. I clutched it in both hands and ducked in back of it.

Great, I thought.

But not good enough for Sir Thomas.

"Choose!" he roared again.

His command made the conservatory windows rattle.

I dodged out from behind the shield long enough to grab the handle of a mace.

I held the shield in my left hand. I balanced the mace in my right. They weighed about a ton each and my arms ached just trying to hold on to them. How could I ever fight?

Would I even get a chance to try?

Sir Thomas threw his head back and laughed.

The battle had begun.

Lucky for me, I'm fast when I have to be. Even in reverse. My feet skidded on the tile floor as I slid backward. I peered over the top of the shield. I saw Sir Thomas pull his mace back, over his head. Then swing it toward me.

The pointy spikes glistened as the mace streaked through the air. I yelped and pushed the shield up in front of me. I ducked my head and braced myself.

Direct hit.

My bones shook as the mace crashed into my shield. A shower of sparks flew off the shield.

And then I heard a horrible cracking sound.

I knew it meant only one thing.

My crumbling shield wouldn't last much longer.

I squeezed my eyes shut.

Sir Thomas had won.

I held my breath. I counted my pounding heartbeats. I knew they'd be my last.

In two seconds I'd be face-to-face with the evil knight. With no shield to protect me.

One. Two. Two and a half.

Two and three-quarters . . .

Nothing happened.

I opened one eye. I opened my other eye.

I checked out my shield. Not a crack in sight.

I spotted Sir Thomas a few steps in front of me. He stared down at his mace.

I stared at it, too.

What remained of it.

When it struck my shield, Sir Thomas's mace

shattered into about a million little pieces. The sharp metal spikes scattered all over the floor.

While Sir Thomas looked closer at the ruined weapon, I peered at the front of my shield. The mace had made a big dent in it, all right. But nothing more.

"Wow!" I couldn't believe my luck.

What was going on here?

Sir Thomas snarled. The red glow behind his visor flared. He hurled his useless mace into the corner. "Wow?" he mimicked. "Do not try your magic words on me, vile creature!"

I spotted his broadsword, gripped in his other metal hand. He sliced the air with some practice swipes as he stomped toward me. The long silver blade flashed in the darkness.

I ducked down and ran for it.

Go! Go! Go! I urged myself.

I couldn't get out the conservatory door. Sir Thomas was blocking it. I pounded through the conservatory. Toward the kitchen. Sir Thomas pounded the floor one step behind me. I threw down the heavy shield. My legs pumped until every muscle ached. My breath burned in my throat.

I heard him close behind me. Closing the small gap. I imagined him reaching out a long metal arm and snagging me by the neck.

I ran even harder.

I punched the door open and raced into the kitchen. My slippers skidded on the tile floor. My feet flew out from under me.

I flailed my arms, trying to keep my balance. Too late. With a painful thud, I landed on my belly and kept sliding.

I heard Sir Thomas's sword whiz through the air above me.

Right where my head would have been.

Our kitchen has one of those islands in it. The kind of counter that stands in the middle of the floor. Regular people use it to cook and serve food. Dad uses it for cleaning weapons.

Scuttling like a beetle, I crawled behind the island. I hopped to my feet and darted to the other end of it, just beyond Sir Thomas's reach.

From my side of the counter I stared over at the knight. The space behind Sir Thomas's visor glowed with bloodred fire. Angry orange sparks shot out from the center of the crackling flames.

What could I use to fight him? I frantically scanned the room. The chains hanging on the wall? Too far away. The broadsword hanging beside them? Too heavy for me even to lift.

Then I saw it.

The catapult.

It stood between me and the door. I could dart over to it and take cover before I dived for the door.

If I could make my feet move.

Fear rooted me to the floor. I felt numb. Paralyzed.

Sir Thomas knew it. The fire in his eyes blazed. He raised his broadsword and whacked it down.

I darted out of the blade's path. Just in time.

The huge blade sliced clean through the countertop.

I crouched behind the catapult and gasped for breath.

With a growl Sir Thomas yanked his sword out of the counter. He swung it from side to side.

With his armor creaking and rattling, he marched toward me.

I could either die here behind the catapult or make one last, desperate dash for the door.

I spun around, all set to go for it.

My hand hit the lever that operated the catapult.

I heard a *boing*ing sound and a *whoosh*. Dad kept a papier-mâché rock in the catapult. I watched it sail toward the knight. I knew it couldn't hurt him, but maybe it would distract him long enough for me to sneak out the door.

It struck him square in the chest.

I dashed to the door. But out of the corner of my eye I saw Sir Thomas stagger back. His arms flew up from his sides. His broadsword and shield clattered to the floor.

The knight raised his head. He looked right at me. The fire in his eyes exploded like lava in a volcano.

Then he fell back onto the floor with a terrible crash.

Knocked out cold.

10

Knocked out? From a papier-mâché rock?

No way.

I came out from behind the catapult really slowly. I stared down at him.

His motionless legs and one arm stuck out from his body at weird angles. His other arm had dropped near the door.

His helmet was tilted to one side. I peered into the slit above his visor but saw only a cold black shadow.

Right in the middle of his breastplate I saw a huge dent.

The knots in my stomach untied. I dragged in a deep breath. It felt like the first one I'd taken in hours.

I spotted the rock under the kitchen table and picked it up. Light as a feather. As always.

A papier-mâché rock couldn't knock out a knight in heavy armor.

But it did!

And I beat the ghastly ghost!

"Yes! Way to go!" I cheered out loud for myself.

"He's lean. He's mean. He's Mike Conway! Undefeated champion—" I announced in my sportscaster's voice.

"Mike?" Dad called from the hallway. He came into the kitchen with Carly. "What's going on down here? Why aren't you in bed?"

Before I could get a word out, Dad flipped on the light.

He gasped. His face turned white. He stared down at the mess of armor on the floor. His mouth hung open.

Then he looked at me.

What a look!

Sir Thomas hadn't killed me. But it looked as if Dad wanted to. Real bad, too.

"Michael Conway! Didn't I tell you to keep your hands off that armor?"

"Now, wait a second, Dad. It's not what you think—"

"It was the bats," Carly piped up. She had on her I-told-you-so face. She crossed her arms over her chest.

"I told you about the bats, Dad. Mike was so afraid of them, he probably ran all over the place, knocking everything over. Including the armor."

"Shut up, Carly. What do you know?" I said. "It was Sir Thomas, Dad," I tried to explain. "He was chasing me all over the place. He called me a wizard. He tried to smash me with his mace, and then he chased me with his sword—" I was speed talking, but I couldn't stop. I wasn't even sure if Dad understood a word I was saying.

"And then, he—"

Suddenly Dad didn't look so sleepy anymore. Behind his glasses, his eyes opened wide.

"The knight? It was him?" Dad grabbed my shoulders. I stopped talking and took a breath. "He made that racket?"

I nodded wildly. Finally he heard me.

"That's wonderful!" Dad said.

"No, Dad. You don't understand."

"You mean he's really haunted?" He stared down at Sir Thomas again. He scooped up the arm that had fallen near the door. He waved it in the air. "What news! What wonderful news! Kids, do you know what this means?"

I darted in front of him. He still didn't understand!

"Dad, listen. The armor's not just haunted. It's dangerous. The knight tried to chop me into a million pieces. He tried to—"

I might as well have told the story to the wall.

Dad didn't hear a word I said. I had never seen him so excited.

"This is great! Better than great! The armor really is haunted. Carly. Mike." He turned to us. "You're looking at the most brilliant man on Fear Street. We'll make a mint. We'll . . ."

He went on and on like that. The more he went on, the lower my shoulders sagged.

"Did he really come down off his horse by himself, Mike?" he asked me. "Did he walk? Did he say anything?"

"Yes, he walked! Yes, he talked!" I yelled at Dad. "And then he tried to slice me in half with a huge sword!"

I never yelled at Dad. We weren't allowed. But this was an emergency.

If he would only listen for two seconds.

I snatched the sleeve of his gray robe.

"Dad, the ghost is here—now. The curse is on us. Whoever owns the armor is doomed. You've got to believe me!"

Dad laughed. He still didn't get it. Or maybe he thought I was acting so crazy because I'd seen a ghost.

His eyes glittered. He rubbed his hands together. "We can add an addition next spring. We'll have to, there will be so many customers."

"But, Dad. Dad, I—"

Dad slipped one arm around my shoulders. He grabbed Carly with the other one. He pressed us both into a huge hug. "We did it!" he said. "We saved the museum! Thanks to Uncle Basil, we've got our very own ghost."

Dad nudged us toward the stairs in the living room. "Well," he said, "I think that's enough excitement for one night. Or should I say one k-n-i-g-h-t?" He laughed at his own joke.

I didn't.

My heart sank. So did my hopes of making Dad listen.

He flicked off the kitchen light. He led us out of the museum. Dad and Carly headed up the steps. He kept talking a mile a minute. "The media, that's what we need. I'll call the TV stations in the morning. And the newspapers. We'll set up a grand opening. A grand unveiling of the haunted knight! This summer the tourists will be waiting in a line a mile long."

Still chuckling, I heard Dad tell Carly good night. Then I heard the sound of his bedroom door closing gently behind him.

Left alone, I kicked at the bottom step. Now what? I had to do something. But I couldn't figure out what.

It was no use.

I was too tired.

And too worried.

There was nothing to do but head back to bed.

I stood at the top of the steps when I thought I heard something. Something that didn't sound right.

I listened hard.

I heard it again. Louder this time.

The short hairs on the back of my neck stood up on end.

I recognized the sound.

The ghostly *clip-clop* of a horse's hooves.

The next day I rushed straight home after school. I dumped my backpack in the upstairs kitchen and grabbed some cookies. Then I ran into the museum, looking for Mr. Spellman.

Dad wouldn't listen to me. But I knew Mr. Spellman would.

I found him in the conservatory working on Sir Thomas. I saw the armor in one piece again stretched out flat on the floor next to the horse. Mr. Spellman was polishing the knight's broadsword.

He turned and smiled when I ran in. "Home from school already, Mike?" he said.

"Mr. Spellman, there you are. Dad wouldn't listen to me last night. But maybe you can warn him."

Mr. Spellman's bushy eyebrows shot up. "Warn him? About what?"

"The armor! It's haunted. Just like the story you told me," I gasped.

"That's what your dad said." He nodded. "He's making big plans for the grand opening next weekend."

"Oh, no!" I collapsed onto the floor. I shook my head. "I hope it's not too late," I said.

"Too late for what? What's wrong, pal?" Mr. Spellman sat down on the floor next to me. His old knees creaked.

I drew in a deep breath. Finally someone would listen to me. Everyone would be safe from Sir Thomas.

Even if it did ruin Dad's grand opening.

Sitting there on the floor, I told Mr. Spellman the whole story, start to finish. His blue eyes widened as he listened. He nodded a few times. But he didn't interrupt me once.

When I finished, Mr. Spellman didn't make fun of me, like Carly did. He didn't get all excited, like Dad did.

He just nodded his white head again. He pulled on his mustache. He was thinking really hard. After a little while he hoisted himself to his feet. He offered me a hand up.

"Mike, you should be proud of yourself," Mr.

Spellman said. "You fought the knight. You beat him. You broke the curse!"

"Do you really think so?" I asked. "But what if Sir Thomas comes back? What if I didn't break the curse? What if he's just waiting for the right time?"

"Hmmm." Mr. Spellman tugged on his mustache again. "I don't know, Mike. It sounds as if you put his evil spirit to rest for once and for all." Mr. Spellman glanced over at the armor. "He looks pretty harmless now, doesn't he?"

I looked at the armor, too. Last night, lit from within with Sir Thomas's ghostly red fire, it had terrified me. Right now in the sunlight the armor did seem harmless.

Maybe Mr. Spellman was right. Maybe I had defeated the knight for good.

But then I remembered Dad's big plans.

All the reporters. All the tourists.

Everyone expected a ghost.

"But what about Dad's big plans? No ghost, no grand opening."

"Yes, you've got a point there." He scratched his head. "Too bad your dad has invited every reporter in town."

"Every reporter?" I echoed.

"TV, radio, newspapers. The works." Mr. Spellman nodded. "He'll be crushed if there's no ghost." He sighed.

I sighed, too.

"Yeah, he'll be crushed," I said.

Mr. Spellman turned to me slowly. "Maybe we shouldn't tell him."

"We shouldn't?"

"Well, when you think about it, what good will it do? No one can guarantee when a ghost will show up anyway. Let the reporters come." He smiled. "The museum could use the publicity, right?"

"I guess so. That makes sense."

"Why upset your dad and ruin his plans?" Mr. Spellman continued in a low voice. He glanced at the armor again. "And who knows—Sir Thomas might return just to be on the five o'clock news."

I grinned. "That would really be something."

"Sure would." Mr. Spellman smiled back.

"I guess you're right," I said. "We won't tell Dad."

"We won't tell anyone," Mr. Spellman agreed.

I nodded. "But I'll keep an eye on Sir Thomas."

"Me, too." Mr. Spellman patted my shoulder. "Now I must get back to work. Want to help put Sir Thomas on his horse?"

I stood up and gazed over at the armor. I put my hands in my pockets.

"Uh—well, I really want to—" I stammered. "But I need to study for this huge math test."

Mr. Spellman chuckled. "Sure thing, Mike. Maybe next time."

He smiled and winked at me.

* * *

That night I couldn't sleep. I leaned back against my pillows and gazed into the blue pendant. And worried.

I worried that Sir Thomas *would* return. He'd charge through the museum and make confetti out of all of us.

Then I worried that the ghost was gone and Dad's grand opening would be a flop. And the thought almost made me wish the ghost would return.

I worried so much that I almost didn't hear it.

Thump. Thump.

I sat up. I listened.

Thump. Thump.

"Very funny, Carly." Grumbling, I got out of bed. "How dumb do you think I am?"

I went downstairs. The sounds grew louder. I followed them. Right back to the kitchen.

"The kitchen? Again?" I shook my head in amazement. Carly didn't have much of an imagination.

Without bothering to turn on the lights, I walked through the museum and into the kitchen.

Thump. Thump.

I heard it, louder than ever. But I didn't see Carly. Anywhere.

For a couple of seconds I stood stone still. I didn't take a breath. I didn't move a muscle.

Until somebody grabbed my arm.

I shrieked and jumped out of my slippers.

"Sorry, Mike."

Mr. Spellman! As soon as I saw him, I relaxed. But not for long.

Something was up.

Mr. Spellman put one finger up to his lips. "I didn't mean to scare you," he whispered. "I was working late in the mummy room when I heard the sound. What do you suppose it is?"

I shrugged. "Probably Carly. She has a rotten sense of humor."

Mr. Spellman crept over to the door of the conservatory. He peeked inside. "It sounds as if it's coming from in here. What do you say? Should we investigate?"

I swallowed hard. My tongue felt thick. My mouth felt dry.

"But, Mr. Spellman," I began, "what if—"

Mr. Spellman didn't let me finish. He gave me a reassuring smile. "Don't worry, Mike. We'll be really careful. I believe you about the haunted armor. I'm not going to take any chances. Not with a ghost as evil as Sir Thomas. Nothing will happen to you. I promise."

I'm not a chicken. But I know one thing. I never would have had the nerve to check out that noise without Mr. Spellman. I followed him into the conservatory.

The second we set foot inside the door, the thumping noise stopped.

Mr. Spellman made sure I stayed in back of him. He led us over to the exhibit.

I spotted Sir Thomas up on his horse. His head facing forward. His lance held high.

Nothing looked out of place.

"Well, I guess we're both wrong this time." Mr. Spellman didn't whisper anymore. He looked as relieved as I felt. "It wasn't the ghost after all."

Mr. Spellman turned around to leave the room. I did, too.

I took one step. Then something whizzed by my head. Close enough to skim my hair.

I saw Mr. Spellman's face turn white.

Then I heard something explode.

A long, thick arrow had slammed into one of Dad's flowerpots not ten feet away. The arrow stuck up from a pile of dirt and the jagged remains of the pot. I knew right away what kind of arrow it was.

It was an arrow from a crossbow.

A knight's crossbow.

Mr. Spellman and I turned around at the same moment.

Just in time to see Sir Thomas charge.

12

~~~

"**R**un for it!" I yelled at Mr. Spellman as I took off at top speed.

I headed for the door. I heard the horse's hooves pounding behind me. Getting louder. Coming closer. Closing the gap between us.

I darted to my right and the knight followed. I veered off to the left. He pulled hard on the horse's reins and stayed right behind me.

I glanced over my shoulder.

Mr. Spellman was beside me. And behind him was the knight.

The red fire behind Sir Thomas's visor was blinding. He held his lance high. I saw the sharp tip. Aimed right at me.

Up ahead the door seemed an impossible distance away.

I pushed myself harder. My lungs burned. I reached out desperately. The door still looked miles away.

Another second and the lance would be right through my back.

I heard a noise. A *whooshing* sound. Like rushing wind.

I braced myself for the blow.

Nothing happened.

I spun around. So scared that I grabbed Mr. Spellman's hand.

All the lances from Dad's exhibit came whizzing off the wall and over my head. Aimed right at the knight.

Some of the lances hit the floor right in front of Sir Thomas and stuck there. Some of them stuck in the floor in back of him. Lances stuck up from the floor to the knight's right. They stuck up to his left.

A cage of lances surrounded him. The knight was trapped. His horse snorted. It stomped the ground.

Sir Thomas let out a deafening roar. He waved his arms over his head. The red flames behind his visor shimmered.

"Wow!" I was flabbergasted. And relieved. I let go of Mr. Spellman. I took a chance and went over to the lances to check them out.

How did this happen? I couldn't figure it out.

That's when I noticed my pendant.

The blue smoke inside the marble swirled and bubbled. Glimmering with a weird blue light. Brighter than Sir Thomas's spooky eyes.

"Wow!" I know, I should have been able to come up with something better to say, but "Wow" seemed to cover all the bases.

It had to be the pendant. It was magic!

Now it had saved me for a second time.

What else could make a papier-mâché rock destroy a suit of armor? What else could make a row of lances fly through the air?

"That's it! That's it, Mr. Spellman. Don't you get it?" I held the pendant up to the moonlight. "You were right! The first time you saw it you knew. The pendant! It *is* magic!"

Still holding the pendant up, I stepped closer to the knight.

Mr. Spellman stood behind me. This time the swords Dad had hung on the wall for display clattered against each other. Battle-axes streaked by in the air.

Awesome!

I could hardly believe it. I tested some more. Waving the pendant, I moved toward the knight.

Sir Thomas winced. He held one metal hand up in front of his face. The red fire behind the visor flickered and faded out.

"Hear me, wicked knight. I *am* a wizard!" I tried to

make my voice low and booming. The way I thought a wizard would sound.

Loud. Important. Powerful.

"I command you to stop attacking us!"

I jabbed the pendant in Sir Thomas's direction.

The swords crashed and smashed over the knight's head. He waved his arms at them. They kept crashing and smashing.

I lifted the pendant up. The round glass orb caught the moonlight. It sparkled. Then it shot a dazzling beam of blue light at Sir Thomas.

As the light struck him, Sir Thomas sat bolt upright.

His armor shimmied and rattled for a second. And then . . .

Boom!

13

His helmet exploded off his shoulders and flew straight up to the ceiling.

A gust of red fire shot up out of the armor.

And then the whole thing fell apart.

Sir Thomas's breastplate clattered to the floor.

His shield fell out of his hands.

And then his arms fell off.

The knight's metal leg guards tottered, then hit the ground.

An awful smell, like burning rubber, hung in the air.

The knight had turned into a pile of scrap metal.

A spooky cloud of red smoke floated above the whole mess.

I held my nose and took a step closer. I heard a soft hissing. Soft, like air leaking out of a tire. I looked down at the pile of armor.

He was gone all right. Gone for good this time.

"I did it! I did it! Way to go, Conway!" I had never been so excited in my whole, entire life. I did a little dance through the last wisps of smoke.

"I really *am* a wizard!"

Then I heard another voice. A strange and chilling one.

"You witless newt! You did nothing. Nothing! I did it all!"

I froze in my tracks. This voice really did sound like a wizard. It boomed through the conservatory. The windows rattled all around me. The floor shook under my feet. The whole place filled with a swirling icy wind that made me shiver.

I spun around, looking for the source of that frightening voice.

"Fool! Do you really believe you possess magic powers?" The voice was coming from Mr. Spellman? Could it be?

He laughed and frosty fingers raced up my spine.

He smiled at me in a way I'd never seen him smile before. A way I didn't like.

His teeth looked pointy and sharp. His skin pulled tight across his face. Like a skull.

Something about his creepy smile made me feel as

if I'd been kicked right in the stomach. I couldn't believe it. I stepped closer to my friend. "Mr. Spellman?"

Mr. Spellman waved his hands. The motion made the air ripple all around me. My skin suddenly felt clammy. I broke out in a cold sweat.

"Do not call me by that ridiculous name, boy!" Mr. Spellman roared. "I am Mardren, the greatest wizard of all time! And now, little bug, I am finished with you!"

Slowly Mr. Spellman raised both his hands. They were covered with golden rings shaped like snakes. The snakes had glowing red and purple jewel eyes that winked in the moonlight. He pointed right at me.

The snake rings came alive. They slithered around his fingers. The snakes grew bigger and bigger. They crawled around his wrists, hissing. Ugly black tongues flickered at me.

A snake head darted out at me. I saw its jaws stretch open and long curved fangs poised to strike.

I leaped back.

Mr. Spellman waved his hands again. The hissing golden snakes transformed into lightning bolts, flashing from his fingertips. The lightning crackled in the air all around me. So close, I felt the lightning's heat as it zipped by my head.

I ducked down. Almost too late.

I smelled burning hair and touched my head. A few strands on top felt hot and singed.

I couldn't believe it. Mr. Spellman. My friend. All this time he tricked me. He tricked everyone!

Crouched down in a corner, I watched as his body transformed.

His eyes glowed. Not red like the knight's. White. Cold. Icy. Hard.

The skin on his face shimmered, like a bowl of Jell-O. Then it turned a sickly yellow-green color that looked dry and leathery. The lines around his eyes and mouth grew deeper and his nose stretched out, long and beak-shaped.

His mustache grew out, too. Long and wild-looking. And his cheeks sprouted a beard. A white beard, all tangled and knotted, that flowed down to his waist.

He waved one hand above his head, and suddenly a long silver stick appeared in his hand.

Then he twirled around, swinging the stick around over his head.

One. Two. Three times.

He spun at top speed, spinning into a complete blur. A purple blur.

I blinked.

He stopped and stood before me. A long purple robe flowed around his body. Purple boots covered his feet and a tall, pointed purple hat balanced on his head.

Symbols that glowed with strange light covered his robe and hat. Silver moons. Golden stars. Strange shapes I'd never seen before.

I saw a big blue circle, too. With swirling blue lights inside.

"My pendant!" I stared at the symbol on Mr. Spellman's robe. I looked down at my pendant.

It softly glowed.

"Mike, Mike, Mike." Mr. Spellman . . . er, Mardren laughed. I felt a creepy, pins-and-needles tingle all over my body. "You really thought you did it all, didn't you?" Mardren shook his head. He smiled a scary smile. "You ridiculous worm! You have no magic power. The power is all mine. I merely used you to destroy my most deadly foe."

Mardren pointed his long silver stick. Right at the pile of armor. With the toe of one purple boot he kicked aside Sir Thomas's helmet. It rolled into the corner.

Mardren chuckled. "Once every hundred years, Sir Thomas and I must fight each other," he explained. "If I defeat him, his ghost is doomed. He must stay a prisoner inside his armor for another hundred years. If he defeats me . . ." Mardren shrugged.

"Well, that is not going to happen, is it? At least not for another hundred years. You took care of that for me."

A memory flashed through my head. I thought about what the knight told me. About fighting the wizard as a dragon. And as a wall of fire.

"You are correct!" Mardren could read my mind! He said out loud everything I was thinking. "Sir Thomas thought you were me. He thought I had taken on the shape of a small, weak boy. It is not what I had planned. Not exactly. But it worked. Why do you think a wizard of my skill and power would hang around in this shabby place?"

The wizard looked around the conservatory. His face puckered up. His nostrils flared.

"With my powers I knew Sir Thomas would arrive here sooner or later. I knew it even before your uncle Basil found the armor in Dreadbury Castle and sent it here. I had to wait for Sir Thomas. I had to fight him."

Mardren stared hungrily at my pendant. His tongue flickered over his cracked lips. He smiled.

A shiver crawled up my back.

"You snatched the pendant before I could, bothersome boy," Mardren said. "That day the armor was delivered you reached first for the magic orb. You touched it first and put it on. There is a spell that gives the pendant its power. After you touched it, I could not take it away from you. No one could. Not until Sir Thomas was destroyed. Now . . ."

A slow smile inched up the edges of Mardren's mustache. He looked down at the pieces of Sir Thomas scattered on the floor. His eyes glittered.

"You took care of that for me. And I never faced any danger. If anyone had to get killed . . ." Mardren shook out his robe. The moons and stars on it flashed at me. "You see what I mean? Everything is perfect now. . . ."

Mardren swung around. He pointed his staff toward me. A single bolt of lightning flashed from the end of it. It shot right at my chest.

The pendant flashed, as if it answered the call of Mardren's magic. It rose right up off my chest. It jerked toward Mardren. It tugged me closer to the wizard.

"You have something that belongs to me, toad." Mardren touched the golden chain with the tip of his staff. The chain snapped. When Mardren lifted his staff, the blue marble globe stuck to the top of it.

"Now I have the magic pendant," Mardren said. "And Sir Thomas can no longer stop me from using it. This magic orb will make me even more powerful." He glanced at the marble. His face lit up with an evil smile.

Mardren looked down at me. "I am afraid I must get rid of you. I cannot allow you to give away my little secret. Hmmm. What should I do?"

Mardren sucked on his shriveled lower lip, thinking. Thinking about getting rid of me.

I swallowed hard. I quietly slid back a step. Run for it, I urged myself.

"Not so fast, toad!" he boomed at me. Mardren's look froze me on the spot. His eyes lit up. "That's it! I know exactly what to do. I will turn you into a mouse. Just be careful! Don't get too close to the cat!"

I caught my breath. It burned my lungs. My hands trembled at my sides.

Mardren saw me shake. Chuckling, he waved his hands over my head. "Keep still, pesky boy! The words of power must be spoken three times." He cleared his throat. His voice rang through the room.

"With the moon over the house, change this boy into a mouse. With the moon over the house, change this boy into a mouse. With the moon over the house, change this boy—"

"Stop!" another voice shouted.

Mardren gasped in surprise.

The voice sounded from the deep shadows on the other side of the conservatory. A deep hollow voice. It echoed. It rumbled.

My heart thumping, I watched a shape materialize out of the shadows. Slowly it clomped forward. With each step I could see more of it.

Metal shoes.

A broad breastplate.

A helmet with an empty space behind the visor.

The knight raised one metal glove. He pointed right at Mardren. His voice boomed.

"Wizard! You will not win!"

14

Sir Thomas. Back again!

The knight lumbered out of the shadows. He took one shaky step forward. Then another.

I stared at the knight—and gasped.

It wasn't Sir Thomas.

One of dad's fake suits of armor had come alive!

"Wh-what's going on here?" I stuttered. Was the ghost of Sir Thomas in *there* now?

I stepped back as the knight clattered forward—his sights set on Mardren this time.

I shot a glance at Mardren. Then the knight. Which one should I run from? Which one?

Before I could move, the wizard's eyes flashed. He

shook his shoulders. He spread his arms. He started the words of another spell.

The knight stomped closer. He swung out at the wizard with his long metal arm.

He missed Mardren by a mile. But one of his heavy metal gloves smacked the pendant on top of Mardren's staff.

The big blue marble wobbled. It teetered. It tumbled from the top of the staff.

Mardren lunged for it, grabbing for the beautiful blue marble as it fell through the air.

The tips of his long, gnarled fingers brushed it.

It slipped past his fingers.

And crashed to the floor.

The glass shattered, and a deafening boom echoed through the room. Louder than a clap of thunder.

A brilliant blue light flashed—flashed so bright I had to cover my eyes.

Then I heard a strange fizzing sound.

The pendant had burst into a zillion pieces. And now some of the shards of glass zipped through the air. Zipped through the air like tiny shooting stars!

Then a cloud of blue smoke swirled up from the floor. Up from the center of the jagged bits of glass that remained there.

It was the most amazing thing I had ever seen.

The blue mist floated over the floor like the fog that

sometimes hovers over the Fear Street Cemetery. It curled around my legs. Everywhere it touched me I felt cold to the bone.

Then it gathered in a cloud around Mardren. It slowly rose up, up, up over his flowing robe.

"No! No!" Mardren screamed. He waved his arms frantically. Trying to wave away the smoke. But the smoke continued to billow.

He puffed up his cheeks and blew at it.

Then he kicked at it with his purple boots.

The blue smoke thinned—and Mardren fell to his knees. Searching. Searching the floor for something.

What? What is he looking for? I wondered, staring hard through the mist.

And that's when I saw it.

A tiny golden sword—glittering in the moonlight.

I blinked in amazement. It must have been hidden in the marble the whole time. Hidden by the swirling smoke.

Mardren grabbed for the sword at the same time I did.

I reached it first.

"Slow as a snail!" I cried.

I snatched up the sword. The moment my fingertips touched it, a jolt of electricity shot through my hand. Raced up my arm. Hit me square in the chest, hard. I staggered back.

My fingers tingled—as if hundreds of pins and needles were piercing them. I didn't care. I held the tiny sword tight in my fist.

Another jolt shot through my hand.

Sparks flew from my fist.

I gaped at my hand—as the tiny sword began to grow, right in the center of my palm.

It grew and grew. Longer. Thicker. Heavier.

It grew until it was the size of a real knight's sword.

I grabbed on to its handle. It fit perfectly in my grip.

I stretched out my arm and waved it. The blade caught the moonlight. It twinkled with the light of a hundred stars.

Then a *whooshing* sound rushed through my ears. And, out of nowhere, pieces of golden armor appeared in the air. Like magic, they snapped onto my body.

Golden shin guards clicked onto my knees to protect my legs. A golden breastplate snapped over my chest.

Golden gloves slipped over my hands. And golden metal sleeves sprang out from them, covering my arms.

"All right!" I whooped.

My voice sounded funny. Echoing inside the helmet that had suddenly appeared over my head.

Holding the golden sword high, I spun around and faced Mardren.

I thought the wizard looked mad before. But that must have been his "have a nice day" face.

Mardren tossed back his head. His lips curled into a sneer—revealing his long, pointed teeth. He let out an ugly snarl. Sparks of lightning crackled from his fingertips.

"So you think you can defeat me?" he howled. A heavy wind whipped through the room, nearly knocking me down. "Nothing can destroy my magic!" he roared.

Mardren spread his arms wide—and started to grow. Into a towering giant.

A huge bolt of lightning exploded from the tip of his staff.

The conservatory lit up with a blinding white light. It hurt my eyes, and I squeezed them shut.

The lightning bolt hung in the air. It sizzled. Cracked and snapped. I could feel its intense heat through my armor—the heavy golden metal singed my skin.

With a sweep of his arm Mardren sent the deadly hot bolt on its course.

On its course—straight at me.

15

I leaped in the air. Just in time.

The lightning streaked beneath me. Inches below my metal shoes.

I staggered back and landed in the arms of the knight.

"Don't give up, Mike." The knight whispered the words against my helmet.

"Carly?" I gasped. "Is that you, Carly?"

"Yes!" she whispered, peeking out of the space between the breastplate and the bottom of the helmet. All I could see were her beady little eyes.

"You distract him," I whispered. "I'll run up and take my best shot."

"I can't see what I'm doing in this soup can," she

said. She pushed me back on my feet. "You've got to fight him alone!"

Then she shoved me forward.

I shook from head to toe. My armor rattled. I lifted one heavy leg and raised my sword.

Mardren stood tall. He sneered a wicked sneer.

I stared into his eyes, about to strike.

Mardren stretched out his arms. He held up a silver stick and waved his arms. His purple robe billowed all around him.

I jumped back.

He tossed his head back and shrieked long and loud. The skin on his face shimmered again, stretching out in all directions. His arms stretched out, his hands turning into big scaly yellow claws. His legs stretched, too, and his body puffed up, like a huge purple blimp.

Cackling wickedly, he floated up from the floor and sailed above me.

I staggered back. My mouth hung open.

I saw his neck stretch out and his beaky nose grow into a long snout. He swooped up to the very top of the ceiling, spinning around in the shadows.

I held tightly to my sword, getting ready for . . . I didn't know what!

I squinted at his dark, twisting form, sailing above me. Then it swooped down. Coming in for a landing.

I crouched down and covered my head.

Flapping wings beat the air and something huge snarled and hissed.

I gulped and looked up again.

I stood face-to-face with a dragon.

A gigantic, hideous dragon with big purple wings.

All over its huge body purple scales oozed foul-smelling slime. Three big yellow eyes rolled around in its head. Two long black forked tongues curled out its mouth. Disgusting green saliva dripped everywhere. The gluey drops sizzled as they hit the floor. The tiles vaporized.

I took a step forward. I swung my sword with both hands wrapped around the handle.

The dragon twisted its ugly head back. The two tongues curled out at me. The dragon sucked in a deep breath. Then blew it out. A putrid cloud hit me. It smelled horrible.

The disgusting stink turned my stomach upside down. It burned my eyes. Inside my armor I gasped for air.

I saw the dragon's huge jaws gape open again. I jumped back and braced myself for the smell.

My eyes widened as I saw a long stream of fire spew out his mouth. The flames licked the toes of my armor boots. My feet were burning up.

"Hey!" I yelped. I hopped from foot to foot. The dragon drew in another deep breath. I readied myself for another huge flame.

"Oh, no, you don't!" I saw Carly running toward us with a fire extinguisher. Dad kept them all over the museum, just in case.

Carly had removed Dad's armor, and she moved just fast enough.

She leaned back and aimed at the dragon. She pulled the lever and fired.

With a *pop* and a *whoosh*, foamy white stuff flew all over the place. The plume of foam shot right down the dragon's throat. It cooled off my feet.

"Way to go, Carly!" I gave her a high five.

When I looked back at the dragon, I saw only Mardren again.

Foamy white gunk dripped off his beard. Globs of it clung to his hat and his purple robe.

His yellow face twisted with anger.

"I am through playing games!" Mardren tossed his staff up in the air. He snapped his fingers. The staff came down again and magically turned into a gleaming sword.

Mardren grabbed the sword. He charged.

"Mike, look out!" Carly screamed.

I pushed her out of the way and raised my sword.

I looked up and there was Mardren.

A sword's length away.

Mardren swung. I blocked his swing with my golden sword. The two blades crashed together.

Sparks flew everywhere. My arm vibrated. It felt as if it had been yanked right off my shoulder.

The next time Mardren came at me, I dodged his sword.

Mardren jabbed low. I jumped. As fast and as high as I could.

By the time Mardren backed off, he was breathing hard. I panted, too. We glared at each other. Beads of sweat ran down my face. Dripping into my eyes. My heart pounded against the suit of magical armor.

Struggling to catch my breath, I kept my eyes on the wizard.

He raised his sword. I saw his lips flicker. I heard him mumble.

Mumble another wicked magic spell.

Mardren raised his sword straight up toward the sky. Purple sparks burst out of the end of it.

The purple fire hit the glass ceiling. It rained down all around us. Just looking at it made me feel dizzy. And sleepy.

Not a good sign.

"Don't look at it. Don't look at it." I kept repeating the warning over and over inside my head.

But I couldn't help it.

Mardren's magic sparks glittered like jewels. The sparks hypnotized me.

"Don't fall asleep now!" I told myself. "You'll be finished!"

I kept blinking my eyes. My eyelids felt so heavy. They drooped, almost closed. I shook my head. My head felt heavy, too. Too heavy to hold up.

I felt my eyes close and my head drop against my chest.

My knees were weak. I staggered forward. My knees buckled.

"No, Mike! No!" Carly shouted at me. Her voice sounded as if it came from really far away. "Don't let him do it!"

I'm not sure how I did it, but I forced my eyes open. The purple sparks fell all around me. I didn't want to think about what would happen if they hit me.

With every last little bit of energy I had, I clasped the sword in two hands and raised my arms.

I propped my sword up on my shoulder. When the sparks got close enough, I batted them with the sword.

Line drives. Grounders. High flies to center field.

Some of the sparks sputtered and sizzled. Some of them bounced. They hit the ceiling and fell down again.

Right on top of Mardren.

"No!" the wizard shrieked. He gave a bloodcurdling scream.

The sparks hit his hat. I heard hissing. Each time one landed on him, I saw a puff of purple smoke rise. The sparks covered his purple robe. They landed all around him on the floor and burst into puffs of purple smoke.

The smoke got thicker. Darker. He tried to move away, but the smoky cloud clung to him. He couldn't shake it off.

In seconds he was standing in a thick, billowing purple cloud.

"No! No! You monstrous children! How could you do this to me?" Mardren waved his arms in the smoke.

Carly crept up beside me. Side by side, we watched the purple cloud cover Mardren from head to toe. And then close in on him.

"No! No!" Mardren's eyes bulged. His mouth twisted in a gruesome scowl.

I could hardly see him anymore. The weird symbols on his robe were dissolving in the smoke. Then his long white beard went up in smoke.

The smoke spread over his face. The cloud covered his eyes. The last thing to disappear was the very tip of the wizard's purple, pointy hat.

"No! No! No!" From out of the smoky cloud we heard Mardren's smothered voice. He whined and groaned. "This can't be happening. Not to me. You evil children! I am Mardren, the most powerful wizard in all the world. No! No . . ."

Mardren's voice got weaker and weaker. Finally I couldn't hear it anymore. The huge cloud of purple smoke swirled around. An awful smell made me choke and cough.

Except for my coughing, the place was suddenly as quiet as a tomb.

Carly and I stood there, listening. Waiting to see what would happen next.

From out of nowhere a cold wind swept through the conservatory. The purple cloud blew away.

Mardren had vanished completely in the smoke.

Or had he?

Right at the spot where the wizard had vanished, I saw something. A huge, hideous purple snail.

"Yuck!" Carly jerked back.

"He can't hurt us anymore." I went a little bit closer to the snail. Bulging red eyes dangled from the ends of long yellow antennae. Thick slime covered a big purple shell. A slimy snail body, a disgusting shade of green, wriggled beneath the shell.

I poked the snail with my golden sword. "Slow as a snail!" I said.

The snail's antennae wiggled in the air, and its eyes bugged out. It tossed its disgusting head. Then it slithered away.

All that was left of Mardren was a trail of purple slime.

16

"**M**ike, you were . . . you were . . ." Carly shook her head. Her smile grew wider and wider. "You were awesome!"

I whipped off my helmet. I couldn't help myself. I smiled, too.

"I *was* awesome, wasn't I?" I waved my sword over my head. I laughed.

"You were pretty awesome, too, Carly," I admitted. "What made you put on that armor?"

"I was going to play a joke on you," she admitted. "But then I heard what Mr. Spellman . . . er . . . Mardren . . . er . . . whoever he was . . . said! I knew Dad was out. I had no choice. There was no way I'd let him turn you into a mouse. I mean, what if the cat ate you? The poor thing would have gotten sick!"

"Thanks a lot!" I was too tired to think of anything funny to say. I'd get her later. After a few hours of sleep.

I yawned and tossed my sword down. The second I did, the rest of the golden armor unsnapped. The pieces clattered to the floor.

I sighed and wiggled my shoulders. I hadn't realized how heavy the armor felt.

"Boy, it's not easy being a knight in shining armor!"

I plunked down on the floor. Right next to the charred pile of Sir Thomas's armor. Now Dad would have to put it all back together again. I poked one of Sir Thomas's shoes with the tip of my sword. I pushed aside one of his gloves.

I set the golden sword down on the floor, between me and the pile of Sir Thomas's armor.

"I feel like I ran a couple miles," I said with a huge yawn. "I can't believe I—"

Something moved next to me. My words stuck in my throat. I heard Carly's muffled scream, but I didn't dare turn to look at her.

My gaze was stuck on Sir Thomas's glove.

All by itself the glove slid out of the pile and right over to the sword. One by one the metal fingers flexed. They closed around the handle of the golden sword.

"Yikes!" I rolled out of the way. I scrambled to my feet.

With the glove still holding on tight, the sword rose in the air. I heard a deep moan. The sound raised the hairs on the back of my neck. The moan started low. And sounded far away. But it got louder by the second. And closer.

Then it surrounded us.

The sword pointed toward the pieces of armor that protected Sir Thomas's legs. With a *whoosh* they rose up off the floor. They floated over to the sword and the glove. They stopped in the place where the knight's legs would be. Next, the sword pointed to the knight's metal boots.

"Mike!" Carly's fingers dug into my arm. "Mike, do something! He's coming back to get us!"

He was! I had to do something. Fast.

I made a diving grab for the boots.

The second my fingers touched the metal, I yelped and pulled them back. The armor stung my fingertips with cold.

I rubbed my hands to warm them. I saw the boots clatter away. Clanking against the tile floor, they marched into place right under the leg guards.

The moaning grew louder. It made my ears hurt. The breastplate flew into the air. It floated into place right above the knight's legs.

The arms came after that. With a clang they

snapped into place where the breastplate met the shoulders.

The other glove flew onto the arm that didn't have a hand. That hand gripped the golden sword, too.

I felt petrified. Worse than petrified. I could feel my pulse pounding against my temples. Hammering so hard, I felt my head about to explode.

Carly and I stared at Sir Thomas.

He stood before us in one piece again.

All except for his head.

With a piercing whistle that made the hair on my arms stand up on end, the sword swung and pointed at Sir Thomas's helmet.

With an answering wail that came from inside, the helmet slowly rose off the floor.

The helmet sailed past us. The air turned icy as it flew by.

The helmet glided over to the rest of the armor. With a click, it floated down into place.

The second it did, the fire behind the visor flared to life.

Sir Thomas's eyes flashed. They sparked. Not purple like Mardren's magical sparks.

Red.

Bloodred.

Sir Thomas didn't say a word. He lifted his sword. He pressed the tip of it against my heart.

17

Sliced to ribbons.

We were about to be sliced to ribbons.

I watched the ugly fire in Sir Thomas's eyes flicker. He stepped forward and I felt the knife point jab me through my T-shirt.

I held my breath and waited to feel his sword run me through.

The knight turned his head. He looked at the puddle of smelly purple slime. Then he turned back and looked at me.

"Who has destroyed Mardren?" His question echoed from inside the armor.

I tried to answer him. But all that came out was a sputtering, choking sound.

Carly pushed me forward. "Mike did it," she said. "He turned the wizard's own magic against him."

The knight didn't move. I could feel his gaze burning from behind the visor.

"Is this true?" he asked.

"Yes," I croaked. "I didn't have much choice. First he tried to turn me into a mouse and then he shot purple sparks at me. But I batted them back at him. With that."

I pointed at the golden sword. My hand shook like crazy. "When the sparks hit Mardren, he was smothered in a cloud of purple smoke. Then he turned into a snail. A big, slimy purple one."

"A snail!" Sir Thomas boomed with laughter. His laugh had a deep metallic ring that echoed through the room. "A slimy purple snail! How fitting for the evil one!"

He laughed and laughed, and the red fire behind the visor settled down to a warm glow.

Suddenly he didn't seem nearly as scary. He didn't seem scary at all.

Sir Thomas knelt on one knee. He bowed his head. "Then, good sir, I owe you my thanks."

"What?" I looked down at his shining helmet. He still held his sword, but now it rested on the floor. "Is this some kind of trick? You mean you've stopped trying to chop me into little pieces?"

Sir Thomas shook his head. "You must forgive

me," he said. "When I saw you with the pendant, I thought you were Mardren. I thought the evil wizard had changed himself into a boy to deceive me. I see now that I was wrong. You were not in league with the wicked sorcerer." The knight looked around the museum. "All of you here, you were never my enemies. You were always my friends."

"Me?" I pointed at myself. A big, goofy smile lit up my face. "I'm your friend?"

"That is correct." Sir Thomas struggled to stand up. In spite of all the oil Dad had used on him, his joints were still pretty rusty. He creaked and wobbled.

I offered him a hand.

This time when I touched the metal, it didn't chill me to the bone.

"I know the story Mardren must have told you," the knight said once he came to his feet. "He told you I was evil. Am I right?"

I nodded.

"Mardren was a scoundrel. A vile and hateful creature." Sir Thomas raised his head. He held it high. "I was never evil. Mardren was the evil one. Many hundreds of years ago I fell in love with his beautiful daughter. He would not allow us to marry. He wanted her to have a husband who was richer and more powerful than I. He put a spell on me, trapping me forever in my suit of armor. I could only be free if

Mardren was defeated. And only one thing could defeat him—my golden sword."

Sir Thomas went over to the purple puddle. He touched it with the toe of his boot.

"But Mardren imprisoned my sword inside his magic pendant," he said. "Even though the pendant remained with me, I couldn't use it. I could never retrieve the sword inside. Without its power I grew weaker and weaker. I knew I'd never be able to fight the wizard. But you did it for me, Mike."

Sir Thomas laughed again. The sound made me feel warm. The way you feel laughing with a friend. "Because of your bravery, I will finally be free of this armor, which has been my prison and my tomb. But first . . ."

Sir Thomas poked his sword in my direction. He waved me closer. "Come here, boy. And kneel."

"I don't know, Mike. . . ." Carly grabbed for my sleeve. I knew she still wasn't sure I could trust him.

But I did trust him. I had a feeling I knew exactly what Sir Thomas wanted to do.

My chest swelled with pride. I went over to the knight. I knelt in front of him.

Sir Thomas raised the sword. He brought it down again, first on my right shoulder. Then on my left. "I, Sir Thomas Barlayne, do dub thee, Sir Michael of the . . . of the . . ." Sir Thomas struggled for the right title.

"How about Sir Michael of History's Mysteries?" I suggested.

"Well said!" Sir Thomas chuckled. "I do dub thee Sir Michael of History's Mysteries."

Sir Thomas stepped back. He held his sword in front of him with both hands. He glanced at Carly. He looked at me. "I will always remember you, my friends," he said. "Now I can rest."

A blue fog rose all around Sir Thomas. It wasn't anything like the purple smoke that smothered Mardren. This was a soft cloud. It hugged Sir Thomas like a favorite blanket. I heard him sigh.

When the cloud blew away, Sir Thomas was gone.

18

"**S**o that's the story. I'm really sorry, Dad. I know how much you wanted a haunted suit of armor. I didn't mean to get rid of the ghost. It just sort of worked out that way."

"That's okay, Mike." Dad ruffled my hair. "I understand what happened. You sure were brave."

Dad put one arm around my shoulders. Carly was standing not too far away. He grabbed her, too. "You, too," he added, laughing. "And just think, all that time we had a wizard in the museum and we didn't even know it."

Carly shivered. "He wasn't a very nice wizard."

"That's for sure." I wanted to shiver, too. But I figured Sir Michael of History's Mysteries would never shiver in public.

Dad grinned. "Wait until I tell Uncle Basil. He's the one who started all this. If he didn't buy Sir Thomas's suit of armor—"

"Mr. Conway!" Someone rapped on the front door and called inside. "Mr. Conway, it's Stanley. From Stanley's Moving and Storage."

Stanley sounded as nervous today as he had the last time he came.

I glanced at Dad. Dad glanced at Carly. Carly stared at me. We all shrugged. Then we raced to the front porch.

When we reached the porch, we all screeched to a stop.

"What is it?" I looked at the huge, wooden crate that Stanley and his helper were lifting out of the van. It had red stamps all over it that said FRAGILE. Stanley and the other guy carried the crate up the front steps. They set it down on the porch. "Who's it from?"

"I don't know." Dad thanked the moving guys. They got back into their van as fast as they could. They were already halfway down Fear Street by the time Dad took out his crowbar.

He worked on the lid, loosening the nails and pushing it up.

Together, we lifted the cover off the crate. The whole box was packed with shredded paper.

"I don't know. . . ." Carly bit her lip. "I don't think

I like the looks of this. I'm sure not sticking my hand in there again."

"I don't like the looks of this, either." Dad took a deep breath. "Well, here goes," he said, and stuck his arm into the paper.

I held my breath.

I wondered what we'd see when Dad pulled his arm out again.

Would it be a helmet with fiery eyes peering out from it? Or a magical pendant filled with blue smoke? Or maybe that yucky purple snail, all slimy and smelly?

Dad pulled his hand out. He held a long white envelope.

"What's this?" He frowned and stared at it. "Should we open it?" he asked us.

But before Carly and I could answer, he tore the envelope open. He pulled out a letter and unfolded it. "Looks like a note from your uncle Basil," he said.

"It is?" Carly and I darted forward at the same time. I got to the letter first.

I snatched the letter out of Dad's hands.

"What does it say?" Carly asked.

I looked down at the letter. I cleared my throat. "It says: 'Dear Barnaby, Mike, and Carly. Well, here it is. The armor I promised you. Sorry it took so long to get to you. I don't know if the legend is true, but the old guy who sold it to me says the armor is haunted. I hope so, don't you? See you when I get back.'"

I blinked in surprise. "Does this mean what I think this means?"

"It means . . ." Dad made a face. His glasses jumped up his nose. "I think it means that wherever Sir Thomas's suit of armor came from, it sure didn't come from Uncle Basil."

"Wow!" I flopped down on the edge of the crate.

"Yeah." Dad said. "Wow!"

"Wait, there's more!" Carly pointed at the letter.

"There's a P.S. 'Mike, there's something extra special for you in the crate.'"

All the color drained out of Carly's face. "Not another magic pendant!"

We all reached into the crate together. We felt around in the paper.

I found the package first. It was soft. It was wrapped in brown paper.

My heart thumping, I tore off the paper. Some sort of white material. A T-shirt.

I shook it out—and read what it said.

"My uncle went to England, and all I got was this dumb shirt."